About the Author

Willem, born in 1996, grew up in the Dutch suburbs. His childhood was spent sailing in the summers and skiing in the winters, instilling in him a deep love for nature. After finishing university, he moved to Amsterdam, where he still lives and works today, finding inspiration in the city's lively atmosphere.

7 Days in Sunny June

Willem van den Berg

7 Days in Sunny June

Olympia Publishers
London

www.olympiapublishers.com
OLYMPIA PAPERBACK EDITION

Copyright © Willem van den Berg 2024

The right of Willem van den Berg to be identified as author of this work has been asserted in accordance with sections 77 and 78 of the Copyright, Designs and Patents Act 1988.

All Rights Reserved

No reproduction, copy or transmission of this publication may be made without written permission.
No paragraph of this publication may be reproduced, copied or transmitted save with the written permission of the publisher, or in accordance with the provisions of the Copyright Act 1956 (as amended).

Any person who commits any unauthorised act in relation to this publication may be liable to criminal prosecution and civil claims for damage.

A CIP catalogue record for this title is available from the British Library.

ISBN:978- 1-83543-275-4

This is a work of fiction.
Names, characters, places and incidents originate from the writer's imagination. Any resemblance to actual persons, living or dead, is purely coincidental.

First Published in 2024

Olympia Publishers
Tallis House
2 Tallis Street
London
EC4Y 0AB

Printed in Great Britain

Dedication

Shout out to all my loved ones.

Chapter 1

It's close to the end of the afternoon and I just got home from a run. Sitting on the couch in front of the window, looking out across the Amsterdam canals, I am sweating my ass of. It has taken a while, but summer has finally arrived. As I am getting up to take a shower, my phone rings. 'Amber' the display reads. It is Monday and I know she has been busy at work.

We chitchat for a while as Amber tells me about her day. She is currently working for a high-flying startup, and as a result of her ambition, she is now practically doing two jobs for the price of one. Never a deal I was particularly in favor of. Even now, I can hear the fatigue through the phone.

"You OK?" I ask her.

"No," she says, almost stumbling over the shitty two-letter word.

"Another three-hour night, incompetent colleagues?"

"Kind of, but also…"

She stops for a second, a pause I have become familiar with. Spending six years of your life with someone, at the very least you get to know them.

"*Hmm*… OK, tell me, what's wrong?"

"I still have doubts."

"*Aahh*… OK… Fuck."

"It comes and goes," she says. "One day I'm excited to be together, but the next, doubts again fill my head."

As such, she kickstarts a conversation we have had

numerous times over the years, in different shapes and forms. Most recently, three months ago when she came back from a two-week-long trip, telling me she wasn't sure about us and that she wanted a break. We have never been the perfect couple. We argue and we fight. We don't like the same superficial shit, which always made small talk difficult. Nevertheless, on a deeper level we have always been strongly aligned. We wanted the same things out of life. Regardless, the message was clear: after being away for two weeks, she was confident in saying she no longer felt that I truly was her 'buddy.' Which I felt was a shitty thing to say, but then again, I have at times been a shitty boyfriend.

At the time, I conceded to her desire to have a break. We knew there was never going to be a magic number, so after some negotiating, we ended up with an arbitrary one month. Time I spent sitting around and waiting. In the end, we had a long talk and decided to try if we could mend things. We, or at least I, made the argument that this was surely the safest route. We could always cut our losses after at least having tried. She agreed, and here we are again.

Talking to her on the phone while sitting in my sweat-soaked running gear, the passage of time allows me to frame the discussion in a different way. We now had two months to reflect, during which at least both parts of the relationship knew that something was askew and that it was important to see if we could steer things in the right direction. Being forced on the phone on a Monday afternoon to look back at those months, there are hopefully insights into the momentum of our broken relationship.

Feeling like everything I had again started to rely on was now slipping through my fingers like a handful of sand, I broke the silence.

"I never expected things to be solved immediately. This was

never going to be a switch you flip on and off. Nevertheless, the last two months have felt nice. I felt like we were at ease. We let each other be while still having fun."

Despite being knocked off my feet, I actually do think we found a better balance, something we can work with. She apparently does not; when I ask if she saw the same progress in the last two months, she is clear. The doubts haven't become less severe or less frequent.

"OK…" I say. "Well that's not where it is supposed to be…"

I never wanted to be in a relationship with someone who doesn't want to be in a relationship with me. Nevertheless, I do think that I at least partly understand what it means to be human, meaning that things can be a bit less binary. Surely reality involves a bit more work than the typical happily ever after fairy tale. For evidence, I could just look at my own quarter-life crisis that fucked up our relationship three years prior, when we were both still in college. Took me a while to figure that shit out. And even longer to get back together.

At the start of our relationship, I could do no wrong, but I often did. One month into dating, Amber surprised me with champagne and strawberries on my birthday. I don't think I ever got to that level of compassion, or at least managed to express it. So when our relationship deteriorated and ended with me saying that I needed time alone, it made sense for me at the time. It very briefly did for Amber too, until she started sending me letters or calling in the middle of the night. I managed to push off, saying that I needed to work on my own crisis by myself. I made it binary. A middle ground would not work. That gave me about two months of peace before I realized I really did want to get back together. But by then, I pushed so hard that Amber was already firmly out of my reach and into some other guy's bed, which stung. It did, however, force some much-needed introspection, and I realized that the balance had been way off.

Trying to keep that in mind, it still felt like shit the first time we went out to dinner together after that initial break, when she told me she slept with someone else, just the night before. Fuck, what a shitty thing to do. Or at least, so it felt. But once again, balance.

So when two weeks in Asia made her confront the realization that I no longer felt like her 'buddy,' it felt pretty fucking awful. But I understood the human emotion behind it and that when everything becomes too much from all directions, be it work, be it social, be it romantic, it can be difficult to attribute blame to the right cause. So after six years of being a meager boyfriend, I could suddenly become the most compassionate man in the land. I sympathized and gave her space to figure things out. However, at the end of the break, she still hadn't figured things out, but my arguments around giving it a go and at least trying not to throw the baby out with the bathwater gave us another solid two months. Two months in which I felt I settled into my role as an above-average boyfriend quite well. But still, my phone had rung. On a Monday.

"How do you feel?" I ask her. "What is different from last time? We agreed that it was going to be work, but that progress would make it worthwhile. Have you not seen any progress then? Because those are different scenarios."

"I don't know," she says, "I keep thinking about everything, going back and forth about how long we have been together. About our plans for the future. About how it can still be fun, but also about how it isn't as much as I hoped for."

"It feels like you're trying to rationalize your way out of this," I said in reply.

A brief silence followed and then a lousy. "Yeah... perhaps."

I always felt like context should not be neglected, to allow for some level of reality. In our case, I was willing to take some hits, knowing that I had mostly dealt them out, and that stress from different places can turn a good relationship sour. Nevertheless, it also feels like once again we have gotten to the point where it is best to make it binary.

Perhaps I also don't want to feel like some second-hand car, where you could try to tally all the pros and cons and make a pretty OK decision based on that. So yeah, he's got a lousy paint job; at least the mileage is decent.

So after another long silence, I now figure it might be best to pull it out of her. Because although it is breaking my heart, it sounds like she already knows, and that the doubts are just a smoke screen covering an inconvenient truth. The reality that our imagined shared future, which solidified over the course of six years, is now in shambles, and that we best start figuring out how to navigate the hundred new scenarios that lay ahead. A lot more alone.

"Amber, I don't think I can do this anymore. I can deal with trying to work things out and giving you what you feel you need. But as long as you don't have a sense of direction, we will never be able to build something."

"Yes," she says, "let's end it."

"OK," I say.

And that's that.

Chapter 2

Being young was the easiest thing I ever did. You are born a hundred different people, and as long as you are young, you can get by dressing up as any of them. On top of that, things are still new and excitement can actually be genuine. You still have things to look forward to, as opposed to merely anticipating planned events. Like birthday parties that feel like a chore, or arbitrary nights out that have long lost their magic. Growing up forces you to start making decisions, and it is at that point that life becomes difficult and scary. I could have been a writer, a rockstar, or just a boring, happy guy, but it feels like the ship has sailed on all those outcomes. I have started to solidify who I am with each and every decision.

Letting dreams die is never easy, but the one thing you get in return is comfort. A fair exchange, trading in endless possibilities for the solace that if you make enough decisions, you solidify your future to such an extent that you never have to make another decision. You will be able to blissfully glide through life, existing within the little framework and set of rules for living you have created for yourself.

A Monday evening can shatter that outlook in an instant. On Tuesday, I already arrive at work a different man. I bleep the security gate open with my key pass and take an elevator up to the thirtieth floor. Arriving at my desk, I am able to look out over all of Amsterdam. A view that is fairly rare in a city with little high rise. My email inbox is as I left it the day before, before I went for that run.

I usually arrive ninety minutes before everyone else. Time I now use to get through my entire inbox. After that, I cancel the reservations I made for the weekend to celebrate Amber's already long-passed birthday. Once that is done, I increase the max daily withdrawal amount from Amber's and my shared savings account. Once that is done, the rest of my colleagues start to drip into the office. Meanwhile, I take my headset and leave for a walk.

I put on some sad hipster indie songs and walk to the elevator. I glide back down to the first floor while listening to some guy sing about how he is 'in love with being broken-hearted.' Sure man.

Stepping back into the sun, I start walking toward the waterfront. From a distance, I can see a bench surrounded by garbage. The bench is placed squarely in the sun, two meters removed from the Amstel River. As such I can understand it is a popular place to kick back, and the large number of beer bottles and rubbish around it almost seem justified. When I look at the bench before sitting down to make sure I don't sit in shit, I notice the plaque on the backrest: 'Paula & Jan 25 years.' Thanks Paula and Jan, for sticking together, because we didn't know how.

Chapter 3

Wednesday morning comes around and sitting up in bed, I am reminded of the need for change. Newness for newness sake can be a powerful tool, but it is not one I have equipped often over the course of the last half-decade. When the collective rhythm of days passes no longer shapes what is ahead of you as vividly as it once has, you are forced back into the wild. With a shattered perception of self that I carefully crafted in combination with a connection to Amber, I am hoping time can once again become my ally. With the future undecided, I am free to again look back at who I was and who I could have been. Past Amber, past the version of me that now exists and into what once might have been. However, as I have tried to shape my dreams to fit my established perception of self, I now question my memories to tell me who I have actually been.

Looking back, love always came easy and early to me. It was only when I actually got to know someone that things became difficult. It is much easier to work with the outline of someone and just fill in the blanks yourself. In doing so, I made versions of women that only existed to me. This has not always served me well, especially because I looked for women to confirm my own version of self, not for who they actually were.

I have never been more in love than at fifteen-year-old, with a girl I only really met once. The night was like magic, and afterward we texted for days. It took her a couple days of texting before she dropped the L-bomb. After that, we scheduled a meet up together with mutual friends, and never have I had such a harrowing, awkward encounter. I don't know if through nerves or just a forced repetition of something that had only briefly existed one night and that we willed into something more, but I don't think we spoke more than fifty words to each other.

My first actual girlfriend was incredible in ways that did not appeal to me at the time. She was bright and happy and brought that into our relationship. A level of compassion once again that I hardly met. As such, we drifted apart and she rightfully broke up with me. Which messed me up significantly more than it should have, given my investment in the relationship. Nevertheless, you don't know what you got till it's gone, apparently really does hit home.

Being dumped but having the advantage of still being young, I tried to craft a reality that incorporated all that I admired at that time. Artistry and the appreciation of the beauty and wickedness of life. All that bollocks. As a young and heartbroken man, I fell in love with a tortured nature because it made me feel interesting. It was therefore that when I met a beautiful redhead who could recite poetry and dressed up like Audrey Hepburn, fireworks erupted. I finally felt like I was in a movie myself. Things were thrilling. Her skin was like porcelain. She made me cocktails from foreign lands and matched my passion like for like. Nevertheless, I was never in love with her. She told me she was with me, which made me feel like a conquering hero. She had a smile men could go to war for. I, however, never really felt strongly about anything, so perhaps that was wasted on me. Even more so, looking back, somewhere between her version of me and reality, I was mostly just a little misguided jerk. Using a beautiful and tender-hearted girl like a prop on a stage.

With all that racing through my mind like a fever dream, I drag myself out of a sweat-soaked bed. Into the shower, back to the tower looking over Amsterdam, the elevator up and then down, and finally back to bed with hopes of kinder dreams.

Chapter 4

Summer typically means a slowdown on multiple fronts, so work has been kind to me today. I manage to squeeze out early, and when I get back home, the sun is still high in the sky. I lock my bike to the canal bridge rail and walk down to the stately canal house I live in together with several friends from college. My motorcycle is parked next to the front door, and looking at it, I think, *God, that is a very cool motorbike.* I don't know if by extension that also makes me cool, but I reason that it is at least better than having no motorbike. Or an ugly motorbike. Perhaps that is even worse.

I have always dreamed of road-tripping on a motorbike. Driving through mountains, deserts, and plains. Setting up a tent each night at a different place but under the same stars. Rugged living, very cool. Then driving into the cities for the weekend, strategically timed, to see what kind of adventures you can find there. Now that I no longer have a significant other, I perhaps have finally run out of excuses to not go on such a trip. I think of Morocco, Norway, Spain, and France. All great destinations for my envisioned trip. I have been to them all and enjoyed each of them for different reasons.

The first time I truly went out on my own, albeit in a Chrysler Voyager, was to France. I was seventeen, and together with three friends, we planned a road trip that would take us from where we grew up to Paris, Biarritz, Montauban, and then Paris again. Man, I love road trips. I love traveling. Sitting in a car, a train, or a boat is the only time you can truly relax and let your mind drift. That's because you're not obliged to do anything. You don't have to answer emails, call your mother, or do the laundry. You're already doing something. Traveling. Going from A to B. And you don't have to do two things at once; that's overkill. Yet the beauty is you're not really doing anything; you're just looking out of a window as the world changes around you. That really does make for the best daydreams.

Nevertheless, it isn't always smooth sailing. Once we reached the heavy Parisian traffic, about thirty minutes in, the locals started to honk at us. It took us a while to figure out why. It turned out that smoke had been coming from all ends of our car. As soon as we figured that out, David pulled the car over, coming to a standstill on a dirty French sidewalk. Afraid that we had broken the car David's dad had so kindly lent to us, we popped the hood to have a closer look. Like we knew what to look for. August was the first to phone a local garage, which advised us to slowly drive over.

"Can you fix it?" August asked the short and bald little French man.

"*Oui, probablement.*"

All right. Our French adventure was officially underway. We would only stay in Paris for two days before heading down to Biarritz, so we quickly headed for our cheap hostel to drop our bags. The hostel, however, was quite far removed from the garage where we left the Chrysler. Being young and not wanting to waste money on a taxi, David suggested we use the weird-looking rental bikes you could pick up and drop off at designated places in the city. Sounded like a decent plan. We all got one and put our bags in the little basket that was attached to the handlebars. The only thing was that three of us had actually brought bags. Steven, however, had not brought a bag. Instead, he had stuffed all his gear in a plastic trash bag. Nevertheless, we already settled on the bikes, so Steven also placed his trash bag in the little basket. What he, however, did not do was tie the bag closed. When we arrived at the hostel, that turned out to have been a poor decision. Apart from having all his stuff for the entire week stuffed in a dodgy-looking trash bag, he had now also lost both his phone and wallet. Both he had placed on top of the pile in the basket, and both had most likely fallen off while we were riding alongside the Seine. As a natural response before admitting he had lost them, Steven had emptied the entire trash bag across the hostel lobby floor, in an effort to find his lost items. That, of course, wasn't a success, so while Steven went to retrace the route we had cycled, we settled in the lobby to fill out the sign-up forms. August took it upon himself to fill out Steven's form. When August started laughing, we asked him what was up.

"The occupation box, *haha*, look."

I looked at the form and in the occupation box for Steven, it read 'magician.' I now also started laughing. We were young and dumb and sitting in a French hostel lobby with clothes scattered all over the floor, so we were feeling a bit jolly.

August went to hand in the forms, and when the cute receptionist who had been watching the entire scene now looked at him, and then to the form, August said, "You get it? Magician, because he made all his stuff disappear."

The little French receptionist was kind enough to return a slight chuckle.

Steven didn't really appreciate the joke. But nevertheless, we were off to a good start.

We had managed to book a simple room with a bunch of bunk beds, just for us. No additional hippy backpackers or lost teenagers would join our dirty little hostel room. That first night was as successful as it probably could have been. Steven had asked his cousin who had lived in the city for advice. She had advised us poorly. We ended up in the gay district, with 500-ml beers we got from a night store, wrapped up nicely in brown paper bags. We didn't find any luck there.

We definitely had trouble navigating the city. I had been twice before, once with my family and once with school, so I took it upon myself to lead us to a more welcoming part of Paris.

"You don't know where the fuck you are going, do you?" David asked.

David was right; I wasn't, but somehow we ended up in a narrow street with a couple of bars that looked semi-welcoming. We entered the first one and sat down at a large table in the corner of the room.

"*Quatres bieres, s'il vous plait*," August said to the barman. Nicely done.

When we were halfway through our third biére, I noticed a group of girls had sat down a couple of tables down from us. There was a tall blond one looking our way. She was very tall. I started making eye contact, and after exchanging some giggles and cheeky smiles, I signed her to come over. For some reason, she actually did. She brought her friends over, which meant too little room for too many people at our table. Luckily the tall blond was quick to solve a problem and took a seat on my lap. My first road trip, in what was supposedly the city of love and I was sitting in a random bar with an extremely tall blond woman on my lap. Must have made for a funny sight, but nevertheless, I felt pretty good about it all.

Meanwhile, August was managing to entertain the three other girls that had taken up residency at our table. That gave

David and Steven the opportunity to focus on their biéres, which they happily did. At the same time, I definitely wasn't able to strike up a normal back-and-forth conversation with the tall French girl. To my rescue came a guy who entered the restaurant selling roses. That was a no-brainer. I bought a rose for my lady, and that apparently was enough of a romantic gesture after ten minutes of fumbling conversation to start kissing at the table.

That went on for a short bit before August figured it might be good to move on to a new place. We all agreed, and the four Dutch guys and the group of Parisian women went their separate ways.

"Hee, man, I didn't want to make a big deal out of it back there, but did you see it?" August said as soon as we were out on the street again.

"No? See what? What are you talking about?"

"*Aaah, haha…* Sorry, man, I was sure you saw it. I mean, how could you not?"

"What the fack are you talking about? What should I have seen?"

"She had a cold sore on her lip…"

"Oh… shit."

Luckily, we ran into the girls again two bars later, and August managed to ask if the tall one indeed had a cold sore. Apparently, it was just a cracked lip. So far, so good.

When we left Paris, we made sure to avoid the rush hour. It was quite a stretch all the way down to Biarritz, but somehow we made it in one piece. Steven's parents had a small house on the coast and were kind enough to let us stay there on our own. We mostly spent our time there drinking and surfing. The waves were big, and the people were nice.

One night, we were wandering through the little French

town, on our way to yet another bar or club. We passed a group of people and standing in the middle of the group was a very pretty French girl. Our eyes met and when I smiled at her, she rushed over.

She hardly spoke any English, and my French wasn't much better. Yet somehow we managed. I remember how she spoke about how her friend was jealous about the fact that she had run off with me. And that she called me the old Dutch man. I was seventeen. I was actually pretty sure she was older than I was. Once again, that made me feel like I was a lot more than I actually was.

We kissed on the beach, and I asked for her number. I thought she was very cool. We ended up texting for a bit after I left France, but that very quickly stopped when I started talking about the weather. The literal weather.

She is a tattoo artist now somewhere. As I said, pretty cool.

Luckily, that wasn't the only surprise Biarritz had for me. Our last evening, I met a girl who invited me over to her apartment. It was on the top floor of an old building, overlooking much of the historic city center. The view definitely was the most romantic of the night. We were both drunk. Or at least I was. Her English was significantly worse than my French, and I couldn't say much more than how tired I was. It was my first time sleeping with someone like that. I still remember what she smelled like.

After that night, it was time for us to leave beautiful Biarritz. David and August drove us all the way to Montauban, where a French chateau awaited us. The chateau was inhabited by a tiny old man, August his grandfather. Or grand-père, as he called him. We called him Geronimo, although I am pretty sure that wasn't his real name. Nevertheless, Geronimo took good care of us, enough that we were soon able to head back to Paris on our way home. Quite the trip for a couple of teenagers fresh out of puberty.

Norway was an entirely different beast. Only a summer later, and being what felt like a man grown, August and I took an old Volkswagen station to the land of winding roads and beautiful women. The Norwegians are a welcoming people. As one of the last countries in Europe, they actually allow you to pitch a tent anywhere. The only underlying guideline is that you shouldn't bother anybody. That's sound lawmaking, in my opinion. We sure took full advantage of that. We had loaded up our trusty little station wagon with two pop-up tents, a whole bunch of pasta, a gas burner, some wine, and a bottle of Dalwhinnie. The first bottle of single malt I had ever bought.

We marked a couple of highlights we wanted to make, but the road in between was for us to discover. The first night, we drove into what to us felt like the last remaining wilderness on earth. With no camping grounds to guide us, we parked the car at what seemed like an appropriate place to continue on foot. We unloaded our bulky pop-up tents and walked into the thick of it. It took us a bit too long to admit that our chosen location was chosen poorly.

"This might not be it, August."

"Yeah, no, this ain't it."

Back we went, struggling through bushes and over fallen trees, all the way to our Volkswagen. Loaded it back up and hit the road again, feeling a bit defeated until we passed what seemed like a huge wall made of rock. So high, we had to lean out of the window to see where it ended.

"Perhaps, if we climb to the top of it? There could be a sound view waiting for us."

That's the spirit. We parked the car next to the road and made the solid decision to first venture out without all our gear to determine whether or not this camping spot had any merit. Good thing we did because it felt like we were climbing straight up into the air. This was one steep rock. However, as soon as it leveled out, it carried us through a bit of green, which opened up into a breathtaking view. We really hadn't gotten far north by this point, so all the exciting bits were still ahead of us. Nevertheless, that first night we dined on pasta and whisky, sitting on top of an ancient boulder overlooking what felt like the entire world. At our feet, there was a lake stretching into the distance, absorbing all our problems and only reflecting back the evening sky.

Despite the scenery, that first glass of Dalwhinnie was a bit rough. Luckily, I felt like a man who could take on much more than a little burning sensation at the back of my throat. The second definitely was better. After the third, we went to sleep.

From there on, it only got better. One of the highlights we went looking for was the infamous Trolltunga. Getting there would likely be a four-hour hike. We figured it was best to head out early in the morning. To prepare, we found a little camping place near the start of the trail where we could wash up a bit. While we were having dinner, we overhead people talking about venturing up the track.

"I heard the trail is especially poor at the moment. There is still plenty of frozen snow on parts of it, but it has also rained heavily the past couple of days."

"*Hmmm...*" his partner answered, "perhaps best to delay it then? It is a huge effort, even under normal circumstances. Best not to push our luck."

"Agreed."

We hardly agreed. Although these guys looked like seasoned hikers and we were sporting shoes we used to play tennis in, we fancied our changes. We were eighteen and bold. We knew how to drink whisky.

So the next morning, of we went, taking the four-hour-long trip up to the Trolltunga. Within those few hours, you visit a hundred different places. Starting out among steep hills covered in forest, you slowly move into large, open rocky terrain, where streams cut across your track in every direction. To be honest, there hardly was a track. There was a general sense of direction, marked by the occasional painted rock. The Norwegians might embrace the tourism their lovely country attracts, but they definitely don't lean into it. The Norwegians stay true to it all. As a result, you don't find a halfway coffee shop. There aren't even waste bins, nor a paved road to follow. Luckily, you aren't the only one making the journey, which meant that when we reached a snowy plain, which seemed to disappear into the sky after roughly five hundred meters, you could see a clear straight line through it, traced by the brave men and women who had come before us. Once we had walked the line, the path winded down a bit, after which we once again started a steep ascent. Focusing on each step, panting heavily, I only looked up once I noticed that the ground below me started leveling again. After I did, it was hard not to be taken aback. We had been at it for a while. Focused on the journey, the destination now started to appear before us.

The Trolltunga is a large slab of gray rock that reaches out into the icy blue sky, hovering above a huge lake, surrounded by snow-tipped mountains. Like an otherworldly version of Pride Rock, it towers hundreds of meters above the lake that lies beneath it.

I wanted to sit on its edge.

Walking out over the roughly three- to four-meter-wide rock, I got close to the point that stretched farthest into the summer sky. As I did, I slowly lowered myself until I was sitting on my behind. Leaning back on my hands, with my legs stretched out in front of me, I slowly edged my way to where the rock ended. Inch by inch, I moved until my feet went over. From that point, I gave it another inch or two until my legs were dangling in the big emptiness. Leaning back as far as I could, I relaxed for a second. I never looked down. I only looked up. It felt good sitting there.

Feeling like we had conquered the entire Scandinavian peninsula, we slowly moved our way east to Oslo, having already visited Bergen in the west. Here, we really got to know the Norwegian women. They are magical. I was always under the assumption that the Swedes were the most beautiful people in the world, but even the Swedes acknowledge the Norwegian superiority. Beautiful faces with chiseled features. Tall and fair, blond, and for some reason, they all seem to sport a very nice tan. Even though the sun tends to play hide and seek for the majority of the year.

As a cherry on top, the Norwegian women all seemed to detest Norwegian men. Apparently, they disapprove of their overly feminine characteristics, focusing too much on skinny jeans and hair gel. Definitely a good place to fall in love. I definitely did a couple of times.

Down south, Morocco is supposedly beautiful. I know there are regular motor trips through the desert and the mountains. What I have seen of the country is a lot more limited. Four days in Marrakech.

Our first night we got local hash the size of a brick. Afterward I am pretty sure we weren't sober for a single second until we got on the plane headed back for Amsterdam. Four days definitely were enough, as the tiny winding streets of the old town and the strong local hashish made for a fairly paranoid vibe.

Thinking about all of that, perhaps it is time for something new. I walk past my motorbike and through my front door.

First, let's see how my hometown treats me this weekend

before I try to turn my life into a Jack Kerouac novel. I didn't even like his book that much. It has its moments, but in between, it is rather thin. Also, I am no Dean Moriarty.

Chapter 5

Friday typically isn't the day I put in the most hours at the office. I usually give it my all in the first four days of the week. Friday, for me is then mostly waiting for the weekend to actually arrive. For now, there are still a couple of emails I get out of the way. Ten a.m. That's it for work, I guess. I don't mind—not today. Today, I don't give a fuck.

Normally, I have no problem entertaining myself alone in my room. I have a large pile of books I can go through. Currently, I am alternating between a *History of the Netherlands* and a collection of short stories by Bukowski, *Tales of Ordinary Madness*. However, reading takes a bit of effort.—More than I am currently able to muster. I don't really care to read about long-dead Dukes, and life is currently depressing enough as is. I don't need Bukowski to drive home that point. So instead, I just settle into my chair and try to figure out how to shape my weekend. While doing so, my phone buzzes. Amber's mom.

"I am sorry to hear about you and Amber. We all hoped and expected it to go differently. Stay strong. Love, Amber's mom and dad."

Thanks, Amber's mom. I guess I thought so too.

Perhaps a drink tonight is a good idea. In the summer, I tend to gravitate toward rum. I forcibly learned by myself to drink whiskey when I was eighteen. Rum came a bit later and a bit easier. Back when I was staying in Surinam for several months. As part of a minor for my bachelor's, myself and a bunch of other students were tasked to reinvigorate a socially and morally dying remote village. The village was roughly a two-hour boat ride from the nearest place that you could actually rightfully call a village. The village's problem was that all the young people were leaving their little sanctuary in the jungle in favor of something more in the big city. I think for them, it usually ended up being just something different, not necessarily more. Nevertheless, the small village was quickly running out of people.

Our university coordinator pushed us to try and implement new agricultural initiatives. When we got there, it very quickly became apparent that the village people didn't care much about more beans in the ground. They could hardly sell them, and there are only so many beans a man can eat. Trying to figure out what could work was mainly based on discussions we had with the village elders.

Speaking on behalf of the community was Booisja, a sixty-something blind man. He had become blind as a result of a large branch covered in long thorns falling on his head. Surinam, as it turned out, could be a cruel place to live. Nevertheless, Booisja's spirit was still high. He cared deeply about his little village and the future of the people living in it. As such, we were keen to help him.

We quickly learned that trying to start a meaningful dialogue with him worked best when we arrived with a bottle of local rum in hand. The little blind man would almost jump up in delight. That is, after we told him what we brought, as he, of course, could not see.

After carefully opening it, he would chant in his local tongue, paying respect to what we thought were the spirits of the jungle. When he was done, he would pour a little of the gold liquid on the floor of his small veranda. For the spirits to enjoy.

Immediately afterward, he would pour himself and all of us a glass. Rum is great stuff. Nowadays, I do prefer it in a glass with a lot of ice, but learning to drink it from dirty plastic cups in the middle of the jungle does have its magic.

During those evenings, we learned that the people in the village were keen to attract tourists. People they could guide around their part of the jungle, cook and care for. We always enjoyed our stays there, so we figured it could work. As such, over the course of the next two months, we went to work, trying to create a place where tourists from Paramaribo could safely arrive. This meant that we stayed with them in the jungle for longer periods on end. In doing so, we quickly fell into a completely unique rhythm, largely dictated by the setting and rising of the sun. During our days in the jungle, we would chop trees to clear a designated area. Man versus the wild. A very singular task you could easily wrap your head around. I loved it. Then, when the sun was about to set, we would build a campfire. It was usually around that time that the women of the village would bring us food they made for us. Pretty much always chicken, rice, and beans. One time we got a weird-tasting chicken, which turned out not to be chicken. Nevertheless, we were well taken care of.

After dinner, the light would go out and the stars would appear. Apart from whatever light we got from them and the moon, it would be absolutely pitch black. That would usually be around seven p.m., signaling the end of our day. We would crawl into our hammocks. Going to sleep, we could hear the monkeys rustling in the trees and the river flowing just thirty meters from where we hung.

Hammocks can be a bit tricky, but once you figure it out, you sleep like a baby. People tend to struggle with the way the hammock bends. To fix this, you gotta lie diagonally. That way, you create a level of tension that pulls the hammock semi-level, meaning you don't have to sleep with your body at a ninety-degree angle.

Then, when the sun rises, so do you. It is very simple. Very easy. On top of that, we actually felt like we were making progress with our project. Apart from staying in the jungle, we set up relations with local tour guides and offices. Feeling like we achieved some level of success with our project, and also because that was part of the reason we all chose to do this as part of our education, we decided to schedule a two-week-long trip through the Surinam jungle.

I have to say, the jungle is fairly boring. It all looks alike. Just a whole bunch of bushes. Nevertheless, it does have its moments. For example, there is a large, two-hundred-and-fifty-meter rock somewhere in the middle of it all. Once you climb that and look out across the horizon, all that bush suddenly looks a whole lot more special. Being able to truly take in the scale of it all, it turns into a magical place. Like a green ocean, stretching out as far as you can see. Also, the rivers and the waterfalls aren't bad.

Perhaps the most special place was a very large area that the local government flooded years ago, creating a huge lake filled with little islands. During our trip there, we visited Jack. Little old Jack was the proud owner of one of these little islands. Jack liked a bit of a drink. He also liked showing us around. The second day that we were guests on his island, he took us fishing. With five people in total, we stepped into a hollowed-out tree. Together, we paddled out between all of the little islands and into a very strange world. After a time, we apparently reached our fishing spot. Out came the fishing rods.

The rods were pretty straightforward. We all got a long branch with a rope tied to one end of it. On the other end of the rope, there was a large hook. In the middle of our tree was a bucket filled with water and little fish, fish that were still swimming around. All you had to do was pierce a squirming fish on the hook and throw it out into the water. We were fishing for piranhas.

The challenge was to notice the piranhas nibbling at your fish. You had to time it exactly right. Once the piranha would bite down on the hook, you would have to swing your rod into the air and pull the fish out of the water. Grabbing hold of your line, you would then need to maneuver the fish into the tiny boot. If you managed to do that, Jack would step in with his machete and whack the piranha on its head. Pretty cool stuff.

That trip was a welcome escape. Apart from the few stretches we spent in the small village, we mostly stayed in Paramaribo. The city has its charm, but not much of it. There is one little piece of town where there are roughly three discos. I liked none of them. The music wasn't for me. So I spent most of my time in the casino. I never really liked casinos back in the Netherlands. Far too expensive. It would cost you fifty euros minimum just to play, and I never managed to play for long.

The casinos in Paramaribo were different. For one, there was no place in the entire country where the AC worked as well as it did in the casinos. Also, my euros bought me enough Surinam dollars to comfortably sit at the blackjack table the entire evening. As a final cherry on top, they would bring free drinks to the table. This meant I would typically drink around six to eight glasses of Black Label filled with ice. I used to do the math: if I drank an X amount of Johnny Walker, I could lose a Y amount of Surinam Dollars. That meant I always went home feeling like a winner.

Coming back to the Netherlands, I never went to another casino. I don't think a tourist ever went on the trip to Booisja and his little village. I doubt little old Jack still lords over his island. But I still drink rum.

The thought of rum gives me a starting point to build my Friday evening around. I do figure that a bit of company might be nice. As such, I ask August and Paul to come over for a drink and a bite. They agree, so I'm off to the liquor store around the corner to get a bottle of double-aged rum. Plantation, as it is called. Questionable name, but good liquor.

When August and Paul arrive toward the end of the afternoon, we set up a little table in the middle of the bridge crossing the Herengracht. The way the canal is lined up facing west, between the rows of houses, means that you sit in the sun till late in the evening. As we settle into our spot and break open the Plantation, we get to talking. It has taken a while for summer to arrive, so now that it is finally here, everybody is eager to make the most of it. We discuss the plans everybody has made for the next couple of months.

We are roughly halfway through the bottle when August asks how Amber and I are.

"Not good," I say. "Done, actually."

August and Paul knew about the recent break and the rough patch we went through, so it isn't a total surprise. But still, it hits them as well.

"Shit, that sucks. How are you handling it?"

"Well, not great, to be honest. It was a long time coming, but still, it stings. I don't really know what to do at the moment. You spent six years together, trying to shape your present and your future. When that drops out from beneath you, it is a challenge to find a sense of direction."

"I can imagine," says Paul.

"How did it happen?" asks August.

I tell them how it went. How my phone rang, and how we talked for a while. How I felt like I had to drag it out of her a bit, but that there was only ever one conclusion left. At least for her.

My friends sit and listen, taking it in.

"So you have only spoken on the phone then?"

"Yeah."

"Aren't you planning to get together? See each other one last time; perhaps address some final stuff?"

"No, not really."

"Why not? I mean, six years, you kind of have to."

"I don't really feel like I have to do anything actually. There isn't anything left unspoken. I know how she feels. It sucks, but I know where she stands, and there isn't much I can do about it. For fuck's sake, man, I tried to give her everything she felt she needed. I spent a month feeling like a ghost while she went on her break. She said she didn't want to be with me anymore. I don't want to add anything to that. I finally want to do myself a favor and rip the band-aid off. I feel like shit…"

"Yes, that is fair," Paul chips in. "Listen, man, we weren't trying to attack you."

"I know. I know… thanks."

"You know, I don't think I have really seen Amber the past two years."

As soon as he says it, I realize August is right. Over time, our relationship had slowly emptied itself of everything that made it special. We used to be great together. We used to love seeing each other. Longing to be together. When Amber came over back when I was still in university, she often didn't leave for days on end. Whatever we enjoyed doing, we wanted to do together. Now, looking back on the past year, it is clear there wasn't much left. We had the framework we had built and we lived in it. We spent time together, having dinner and watching television, but that was pretty much it. I spent the last of it chasing after someone who didn't want to be with me.

I had dinner with friends, she didn't want to come. I had a wedding in Italy, she didn't want to join. I wanted to live with her, but she didn't want to live with me. It took its toll. It would be easy to say that toward the end there wasn't much left because I was scared to suggest things, knowing that most likely Amber wouldn't be up for it. That I took a backseat role in my own relationship. I think that would be too easy. I think I should have put the effort in when it still mattered. When we were still close. I don't know if me being a poor boyfriend meant she drifted away from me. I guess that is probably the best reason.

I turn to August and say, "Yeah, I don't think there is a coming back from this."

Of course, I wish we would still be together, but as we were when we were at our best. Two peas in a pod. I know she doesn't love me anymore. She doesn't envision a shared future with me because in the end, she just doesn't want to share her time with me anymore. That shifts the dynamic between two people too much. There is no trying after that. That is squarely back to zero. But without the excitement and potential of a first try. We somehow managed it once. Or perhaps we just postponed the inevitable. Things certainly were different after our first break.

Now, the realization that I have to start over is daunting. I was never really one for excessive dating. Keeping it casual was a lot easier. Nevertheless, Amber and I did it well. On our first date, I picked her up from the train station. We walked to a local cocktail bar and spent the next couple of hours drinking and talking. It was the end of August. After the cocktails, I took her dancing. We arrived so early; we were the first ones there. We didn't mind much. We didn't need much more. I don't know how long we spent in that shady, dark club. I do remember how every time I went to the bar to get us a drink, guys would look at me like I won the lottery. Sure felt that way.

Later that evening, we slept together and the next morning, we decided to go for breakfast. She ordered scrambled eggs. Later she told me that she doesn't even really like eggs but that she wanted to order something modest out of fear of what I might think of her. God, I love that woman.

After breakfast, we went to the movies. Love seats. Great first date. Best I ever had. Second date was the day after. Gin tonics at her place. Day after that, we were walking hand in hand through the city.

With all of that gone, I look out over the bridge, toward the setting sun. We finish the bottle and order some pizza. While slicing up our pepperoni, Paul puts forward the notion that it might be a good idea to move onto skinny bitches. A cocktail which gets its name from the limited amount of calories it has and, therefore, the people who drink it. Basically, it is just vodka with ice, some soda water, and a lime. I drink it for different reasons.

I am not good at managing hangovers. Beer, in particular, fucks me up. Waking up after a night of twenty beers, it feels like I ate an entire loaf of bread. With vodka, or any hard liquor for that matter, that is not an issue. The beauty of the skinny bitch, however, is that you also add a whole bunch of water and ice to the equation. That basically means that for every skinny bitch, you also drink a glass of water. That helps with the hydration, which helps with the headache. Also, I just really like them.

"Yeah, sure, why the fuck not?" August quickly responds.

As such, I jump on my bike to drive to the only liquor store that is still open. I get a bottle of Grey Goose. Very expensive, but worth it. With Absolut, or most other standard brands, it tastes like nail polish remover, and the hangover still sucks. So Grey Goose it is. Then to the supermarket for water, ice, and lime. On my way out, I also get a pack of smokes. I already started bumming smoke from August and Paul, so that's my treat. Nine they charge. Fuck me.

As I pour our drinks, Paul moves the conversation forward.

"What is your strategy to mend your broken heart?"

"Getting through this bottle of vodka is part of it."

"Sound strategy." Paul nods in approval.

"Do you plan on jumping back in? Break the ice and get some separation, distance, and perhaps distraction from what has happened."

"I don't know; to be honest, I really don't have a fucking clue at the moment."

I always believed that if you ever had the urge to cheat, you should just break it up immediately. However, most people don't. In that sense, I think Oscar Wilde had it right: when you fall in love, you start by deceiving others. After a while, you start deceiving yourself. For me, it had always been different. Why be in a place you don't really want to be? There was only one reason I was with Amber. Because I didn't want to be with anyone else. So I don't really know what it is like out there. I haven't flirted in bars for over six years. I have changed, and likely some things out there have changed as well.

For starters, one thing I have noticed is that as I have gotten older, bikinis have gotten smaller. When I was a horny teenager, the bikini in itself was exciting enough. A bit of thigh and some booby outline and you're there. It was definitely enough cloth to cover up most of the exciting parts. Nowadays, if you want to stand out from the crowd, you pretty much have to drag a shoelace through your ass and tie it across your belly. I'll be honest, I'm not sure how I feel about that. The casualness of sexuality sure seems cool, and the underlying trend of empowerment I can get behind. Free the nipple and all that. But still, I am not sure if there aren't also some more darker forces at work. For example, yoga pants used to be every guy's dream. They would strap an ass in tightly and pretty much outline everything you had to work with. But somehow, someday, someone decided that wasn't enough. I would have killed to be in the meeting of whatever sports apparel company came up with this, where some guy must have been. "So yeah, you know how everyone likes yoga pants? Because you can see the entire ass outline? Well, how about we one up that shit? How about we put a BUILD-IN ASS CRACK INTO THAT SHIT! How about that?" Man, that conference room must have erupted. And then, what marketing genius got it out there, in such a way that if you now go to a gym, five out of ten ladies are walking around with their asses visibly clapping through their nylon yoga pants. God it is wild out there.

Perhaps I don't want to have to see everyone's nipple; perhaps an ass crack is still fine, but there has to be a line somewhere I guess? I mean, at a certain point, it basically becomes one big slippery slope before we all digress back into communal living and mass open relations. Meanwhile, Instagram is whatever you need it to be, but to me and probably a whole bunch of other dudes, it is basically a bit of football, recycled vines, and a whole bunch of soft porn. Personally, I like a bit of mystery, and the fact that you can still give things to significant others that you don't share with the general public. Otherwise, what would be left of intimacy? I like the fact that I can see a thousand breasts on the internet, but that I can't see hers. Hers will only appear once she deems me worthy.

As Paul empties out the last of the Grey Goose across our three empty glasses, I start to think of intimacy. There are a lot of reasons to go out into the night, to whatever bar or club that suits your fancy. I have found that most of them revolve around girls. As such, I hardly went out anymore the last couple of years. Being newly girl less, it suddenly again feels like a sound idea.

"Hee, we should go out."

"Where to?" asks David.

"The Pijp, perhaps?" August answers.

"Yeah, let's go to the Pijp."

We quickly finish what is left of our liquid courage and head out.

The first bar we enter is filled with people standing shoulder-to-shoulder.

Following closely behind August, we make our way to the bar.

"Three Bacardi Colas," he tells the bartender.

As the grumpy-looking fellow starts mixing our dancing juice, I look out into the crowded space. A lot of faces. Non familiar. Just what I was looking for. Pretty blondes and brunettes. Or so I make them out to be. The feeling has crept up on me. Somewhere between the Rum and Vodka. I want to talk to a girl, and I want her to take me home with her.

Currently, the only reason I am so keen to end up in a strange bed, next to a strange girl, is to get the feeling that I still matter. I have enough to offer to be taken home with someone. Carnal needs are nowhere to be found. I just need confirmation of my own existence. Turns out, I have some confidence issues. I feel like that tree in the forest. The one that falls to the forest ground without anyone near enough to hear it break into a million pieces. If that tree doesn't make a sound, am I still interesting without anyone to confirm it by jumping into bed with me?

Unfortunately, no one automatically comes up to me to tell me she loves me or just that I am the goodest looking and most interesting guy she has ever met, which she could tell just by looking at me in this crowded bar.

We finish our drinks and head home. Not sure whether I won or lost. Perhaps the question of my own relevance is still a question best answered by myself. Let's chalk it up as a small win.

Chapter 6

The first morning of my new life where I don't have to drag myself to work, and I have somehow managed to make it the worst. I have a hangover coming out of my nose, ears, and ass.

As I twist and turn in my once again sweat-soaked bed, I hear my phone buzz somewhere close to my head. It's August, saying we should get some breakfast. Perhaps we should. I drag myself out of bed, into the shower, into some clean clothes, and out the door. The sun is shining.

"You know how people always say, 'Fake it till you make it'? Well, most people just go through life faking it, never making it. Nobody really knows how to do anything. Or they just don't bother. Getting something exactly right requires effort and attention. Some things actually require skill, but most things only require some level of effort and attention to get right. Even that is too much for most people. It is some weird, paradoxical public secret. Most people know they are just coasting through life, not bothering to get things truly right, but just right enough to get by. Yet, pretty much everyone expects everyone else to get things exactly right. People have binary expectations of things and blindly rely on them. If you walk into a restaurant, people expect a good and properly prepared steak. If you happen to walk into a fancy place, where there is actually a guy in the kitchen making a career out of cooking meat, you might be in for a treat. However, in most places, the kitchen staff, the waiters, and everyone in the building is faking just enough of an effort for the other posers coming to their shitty restaurant to pay for a meal and not complain. This is as true in tiny restaurants as it is in large corporations, in government, as it is everywhere else. It takes effort and precision to get a steak precisely right. You need to time it, the heat needs to be right, you even need to account for different levels of thickness in the meat. Why try to get all of those things exactly right when you can also just roughly wing it and get close enough? No one will die from a so-so steak. Most likely, no one will even complain. Some won't even notice. Nine out of ten people fake their careers, their hobbies, and their love lives in such a fashion. Yet most people are surprised when they find out someone else wasn't putting in a hundred percent. It is crazy, and once you start noticing it, you can't unsee it. It is just a bunch of fakers being faked by other fakers."

"Yeah," I say, "perhaps, I just really want to get some food. I'm starving."

I am generally not worth a whole bunch when I am hungover. Also, at this point, I don't really care if someone isn't going to put their heart and soul into the sloppy burger I am planning on ordering.

Luckily, August and I find our way to the little hole-in-the-wall burger joint we usually frequent after a night of heavy drinking.

"One double cheeseburger and a glass of milk, please."

"Coming right up, darling."

The woman behind the tiny bar is a real piece of work. She is quick to anger when you're not courteous enough. As such, I am always keen to stress the pretty please.

Settling down and watching August apathetically attack his order of fries, my mind wanders to Amber. When I am truly hungover, it can feel like the walls are closing in around me.

There is a tightness in my chest, and I get anxious and uncertain. If I am really feeling it, I can completely lose my ability to express myself and instead turn into a mumbling fool. On top of that, to really make it a horrendous experience, I can get extremely emotional. Currently, it means I am left to reflect on how, among all of the fakers and all of the people that are coasting by on shallow expectations and empty promises, there are a few hidden gems. For some reason, one landed in my lap. There was never a moment in which Amber didn't know exactly what she wanted. I was absolutely in love with the fact that she shaped her world to her liking, because hardly anyone ever does. She was kind enough to let me into that world.

Truly being conscious of your choices, however small, brings a unique dynamism to your life. You can sometimes catch glimpses of it during the simple routines of normal people. When someone strays away from a specific recipe to add an ingredient that is to their specific liking, they experience a thrill that never comes naturally to them. Knowing that they are going rogue in the most insignificant way imaginable to turn a little piece of life into something personal.

For most, that is as far as they come. Amber did more of it. She held herself to the highest standards imaginable, only allowing things to be just right. That is not to say that this was ever only a good thing. She was extremely compulsive, forcing things to be binary. Something could never be OK. It was either the world's greatest thing to ever exist, or it wasn't worth a moment of her attention. That can sometimes turn into a bit of a rollercoaster ride. It definitely put stress on our relationship, as she was extremely quick to drop things and move on to whatever captured her imagination next.

That is perhaps also why it hurts so damn much that she

spent the better part of a year walking around feeling only more or less OK about our relationship, but never really doing anything about it. For a long time, I was probably the only thing in her life she felt OK about.

Luckily, the double cheeseburger doesn't disappoint.

When we get back home, I crash on the couch for a bit. A Saturday can pass you by quickly like that. When I wake up, I decide to take a hot shower to freshen up. It seems to do the trick. I go back into my room, put on some music, take an aspirin, and look into the mirror. My wet hair is slicked back, and my blue eyes stare back at me. A face that people have loved. For minutes and for years. I think it is a decent face. It is not a face that wears a large range of emotions. It tends to sit comfortably in the middle. I prefer to look intriguing, mysterious. When I was little, people on the street used to tell me I needed to smile more. I just thought I was looking cool.

Anyway, the mirror returns a cheeky smile, and I decide it might be a night for dancing.

Night falls, and we decide to go to a place in one of the farthest corners of Amsterdam. A place I love. It is tiny and usually crowded, but not so much that you're constantly pressed against one another. There is room to move, room to dance, which is a good thing because they always seem to get the music just right. Stuff you can swing to. Music with a bounce. Also, they mix a mean drink. Nice and strong.

Tonight, they seem to be getting it right again. The music is soulful and my rum cola is pretty much transparent. The whole floor is moving up and down to the rhythm of the music. I start to inhibit my own little piece of the dance floor. My friends are floating loosely around me.

As I am getting into it, I notice a cute little blonde dancing a couple of meters closer to the DJ. She seems to be with friends, but she also doesn't really seem to notice anything but the music.

August taps me on the shoulder, putting two fingers to his mouth, signaling he is going for a smoke. David and Paul follow him outside, and so do I.

The air outside is nice and cool. The terrace is mostly dark, apart from some dimly lit lights and the tiny embers coming from smoking cigarettes.

As the four of us start to light up, I notice the small blonde coming outside with one of her friends. I notice her friend goes for a pack of cigarettes.

"Need a light?" I say as I offer her one.

"Thanks," the tall brunette says, smiling.

As she cups her hands against the wind, I hold the lighter close to her face to light the cigarette that is dangling from her lips. As she inhales, the flame grows bigger. I look over to my left, smiling. Even in the dark, I can clearly see the big blue eyes of the cute blonde. She smiles back at me. Placing a cigarette between her lips, she moves closer to me so that I can easily light it for her.

While both of them inhale, I put the lighter away and put my right hand forward.

"What's your name?" I ask both of them at the same time.

The brunette is the first to shake my hand.

"Charlotte."

Then the blonde.

"Jean."

"Hello, Charlotte. Hello, Jean. What brought the two of you here tonight?"

The blonde one chuckles. "Charlotte here writes gastronomy reviews. They have a great hamburger here. Did you know that?"

"No," I answer, laughing. "No, I did not know that. But I am definitely happy now that I do. I used to just come here for the pretty girls, but a hamburger sure sounds like a better excuse."

Another tap on the shoulder.

"We're going back in for another round of drinks. You want one?"

"Yes, I'll join you."

I turn back to Charlotte and Jean, who are now halfway through their cigarettes.

"See you back inside?"

The girls smile politely as I head off for yet another drink.

When I am halfway through my drink, the girls reappear on the dance floor. We move closer to each other. I down my drink so I have both hands free. I let the plastic cup fall to the ground. As the music starts to pick up, I stretch my hand out to the tiny blonde girl dancing in front of me. She places her hand in mine, and I pull her toward me. As she leans in, I twist her around and place my hands on her hips. She moves them to the rhythm of the music in front of me. We twist and dance around each other until our faces come close. I lean in, and she moves away gracefully. We repeat that ritual until the song ends.

It is warm inside, and I have worked up a bit of a sweat. I lean in and ask her if she wants to go outside for a smoke. She smiles and takes my hand, leading me out the door and back into the dark.

The night has grown colder. It is refreshing. I walk out onto the terrace and take a seat. Jean takes a seat next to me on the wooden bench. I light a cigarette. Cigarettes make me feel cool, and I am making a conscious effort to look cool.

Jean's face is close to mine.

"I really want to kiss you now," she says while looking into my eyes.

"Well, why don't you?"

"I can't, not really. I am currently still dating someone."

"*Ah,* yes. That tends to get in the way of kissing strangers in the dark of night."

A quick smile.

"I have been planning to end it with him."

"Well, to be honest, I am neither capable nor willing to be your moral compass tonight. So perhaps it's best not to resolve your longing for a kiss?"

Silence from Jean.

I smile.

"Here, my phone. Feel free to enter your number. I'll give you a text, so you have mine as well. Then, when the dust settles, give me a call."

She enters her digits and hands it back to me. I sent a simple text, and that is that.

I move to get up from the bench and as I do, I move one hand past her cheek to the back of her neck. I lightly grab her hair as I lean in to give her a kiss on her cheek.

"Sweet dreams," I say.

As I walk away, over to where the guys are having a cigarette, I start to feel pretty good about myself. I regained some control. About how I feel and about how I act. Once again, a night that seems to end in a win.

August looks up to me and as he exhales, he asks, "No goodnight kiss for the tiny dancer?"

"Boyfriend."

"*Ah*, well, good for you."

I light another cigarette and as I do, we all start to move to where we parked our bikes. I parked mine closer to the entrance than the rest and as I struggle with my lock, I feel a hand on my shoulder.

"What happens when I call you?"

"I don't know."

"How do I know you won't disappoint?"

"I only tend to disappoint once you really get to know me."

"Then how about we just fuck?"

"OK."

She lives a fifteen-minute bike ride away, and we make it to her apartment in one piece. She shares it with three roommates, all of whom are apparently on a holiday. That's nice.

The apartment is cozy and extremely neat. That is something that, for some reason, takes me aback a bit. A house well in order. The drinks probably make me read into that more than I should.

Jean opens a sliding door to a tiny balcony. Time for yet another cigarette. As I make my way outside, she asks me if I want another drink.

"Well, I wouldn't dare to break up your relationship and finish your wine all in one night. I don't mean to be a poor guest."

"There are worse things to do."

"I can't really think of any, but sure, some wine sounds nice."

She comes over with two glasses and a bottle. She starts a story about the vineyard she got the wine from, which she visited with her family. I get into it. Into her stories and her life. And I give back plenty. I am funny and engaging. I give it my all. It comes naturally, but perhaps it shouldn't. I always tend to give too much of myself away. That is the only way I like it.

That is why I was always very comfortable with casual sex. I could really enjoy it because to me, it was never just casual. To be fair, I never tended to look into the future for something more, but I always aimed to enjoy time spent together. And more often than not, I actually did. I like spending time with people I don't really know. And I tend to be good fun when people don't really know me.

    This night turns out to be no different. But when I awake sometime before the sun starts to rise, it feels strange. I get out of bed and walk back to the tiny balcony. As I pass the living room, I see the pictures on the wall. Suddenly, a whole new world opens up to you. A history that you weren't part of. Places that have been visited without you, ideas and motivations you have no part in. It is a strange feeling to dip your toes in that. It also allows you to be whomever you want to be. A role I gladly played tonight. Nevertheless, standing here in the middle of a strange life, I can't help but wonder what the fack it is I am doing. Not really knowing what my own life is going to look like.

Chapter 7

The sun is shining and I take it in. I think of Amber. I think of how we used to be together and how we aren't anymore. How the strawberries and the champagne seem like a lifetime ago. I think about how it seems like I have already forgotten what it was like to be together. That's nice. It took God six days to create this world. So why can't I forget about mine in seven?

Chapter 8

I thought I was OK, but it turns out I am not OK. It is Monday, and I now have anxiety.

I wrestle myself out of bed. After I shower, I walk back downstairs. On the kitchen table, the empty rum bottle still stands. I think about Surinam. Of all the smells, wild animals, and slowly setting suns, what I remember most vividly is how Amber smiled at me at the airport when she came to see me off.

In doing so, in the emptiness of my morning, I find out that cheap thrills and shortcuts are hardly a solution and that sincerity is scary.